THE TALE OF
PETER RABBIT

BY

BEATRIX POTTER

GROSSET & DUNLAP

Published in 2004 by Grosset & Dunlap, a division of Penguin Young Readers Group,
345 Hudson Street, New York, New York 10014. Printed in the U.S.A.

Web site at: www.peterrabbit.com

Library of Congress Cataloging-in-Publication Data

Potter, Beatrix, 1866–1943.
The tale of Peter Rabbit /c by Beatrix Potter ; [artwork by Alex Vining].
p. cm.
Summary: Peter disobeys his mother by going into
Mr. McGregor's garden and almost gets caught.
ISBN 0-448-43521-7 (pbk.)
[1. Rabbits—Fiction.] I. Vining, Alex, ill. II. Title.
PZ7.P85Tap 2004
[E]—dc22
2003017675
ISBN 0-448-43521-7

THE TALE OF
PETER RABBIT

GROSSET & DUNLAP

Once upon a time there were four little rabbits, and their names were:

Flopsy,

Mopsy,

Cottontail,

and Peter.

They lived with their mother in a sandbank, underneath the root of a very big fir tree.

"Now, my dears," said old Mrs. Rabbit one morning, "you may go into the fields or down the lane, but don't go into Mr. McGregor's garden.

"Your father had an accident there. He was put in a pie by Mrs. McGregor.

"Now run along, and don't get into mischief. I am going out."

Then old Mrs. Rabbit took a basket and her umbrella, and went through the woods to the baker's. She bought a loaf of brown bread and five currant buns.

Flopsy, Mopsy, and Cottontail, who were good little bunnies, went down the lane to gather blackberries.

But Peter, who was very naughty, ran straight away to Mr. McGregor's garden and squeezed under the gate!

First he ate some lettuce and some French beans, and then he ate some radishes.

And then, feeling rather sick, he went to look for some parsley.

But around the end of a cucumber frame, whom should he meet but Mr. McGregor!

Mr. McGregor was on his hands and knees planting young cabbages, but he jumped up and ran after Peter, waving a rake and calling out, "Stop, thief!"

Peter was dreadfully frightened. He rushed all over the garden, for he had forgotten the way back to the gate.

He lost one of his shoes among the cabbages, and the other shoe among the potatoes.

After losing them, he ran on four legs and went faster, so that he might have gotten away if he had not unfortunately run into a gooseberry net, and got caught by the large buttons on his jacket. It was a blue jacket with brass buttons, quite new.

Peter gave himself up for lost, and shed big tears. But his sobs were overheard by some friendly sparrows, who flew to him in great excitement and begged him to try to free himself.

Mr. McGregor found a sieve,
which he intended to put on top
of Peter. But Peter wriggled out
just in time, leaving his jacket
behind him.

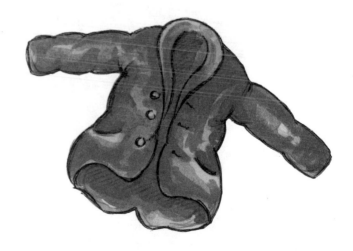

Peter rushed into the toolshed and jumped into a watering can. It would have been a beautiful thing to hide in if it had not had so much water in it.

Mr. McGregor was quite sure that Peter was somewhere in the toolshed, perhaps hidden underneath a flowerpot. He began to turn them over carefully, looking under each.

Suddenly, Peter sneezed—"*Kertyschoo!*"

Mr. McGregor was after him in no time.

He tried to catch Peter, who jumped out a window, upsetting three plants. The window was too small for Mr. McGregor, and he was tired of running after Peter. He went back to his work.

Peter sat down to rest. He was out of breath and trembling with fright, and he had no idea which way to go. Also he was very damp from sitting in that can.

After a time he began to wander about, going *lippity*, *lippity*—not very fast, and looking all around.

He found a door in a wall, but it was locked. And there was no room for a fat little rabbit to squeeze underneath.

An old mouse was running in and out over the stone doorstep, carrying peas and beans to her family in the woods. Peter asked her the way to the gate, but she had such a large pea in her mouth that she could not answer. She only shook her head at him. Peter began to cry.

Then he tried to find his way straight across the garden, but he became more and more puzzled. Presently, he came to a pond. A white cat was staring at some goldfish. She sat very, very still, but now and then the tip of her tail twitched as if it was alive. Peter thought it best to go away without speaking to her; he had heard about cats from his cousin, little Benjamin Bunny.

He went back toward the toolshed, but suddenly, quite close to him, he heard the noise of a hoe—*scr-r-ritch, scratch, scratch, scritch*. Peter scuttered underneath the bushes.

But soon, as nothing happened, he came out and climbed upon a wheelbarrow and peeped over. The first thing he saw was Mr. McGregor hoeing onions. His back was turned toward Peter, and beyond him was the gate!

Peter got down very quietly off the wheelbarrow, and started running as fast as he could go, along a straight walk behind some blackberry bushes.

Mr. McGregor caught sight of him at the corner, but Peter did not care. He slipped underneath the gate, and was safe at last in the woods outside the garden.

Mr. McGregor hung up the little jacket and the shoes as a scarecrow to frighten the blackbirds.

Peter never stopped running or looking behind him until he got home to the big fir tree.

He was so tired that he flopped down upon the nice soft sand on the floor of the rabbit hole, and shut his eyes.

His mother was busy cooking. She wondered what he had done with his clothes. It was the second little jacket and pair of shoes that Peter had lost in two weeks!

That evening, Peter was not very well.

His mother put him to bed, and made some chamomile tea. She gave a dose of it to Peter!

"One tablespoonful to be taken at bedtime," she said.

But Flopsy, Mopsy, and Cottontail had bread and milk and blackberries for supper.